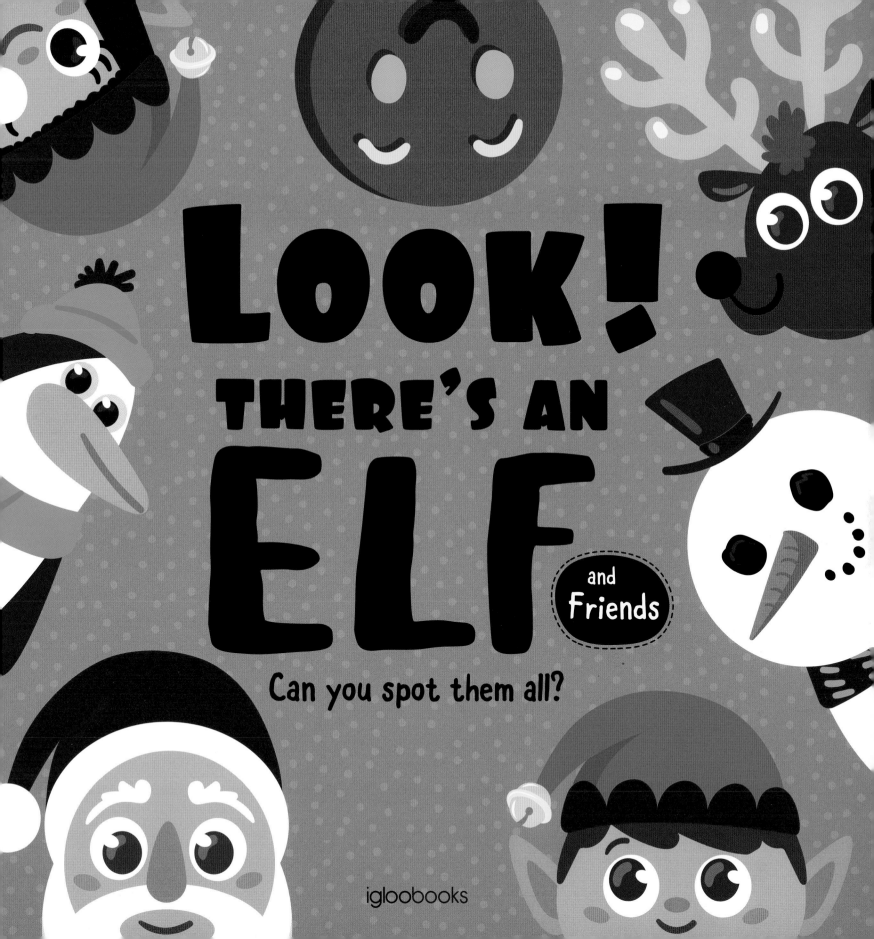

# LOOK!
# THERE'S AN
# ELF.

and
Friends

Can you spot them all?

igloobooks

# MEET THE CHRISTMAS CREW!

**Time for some festive fun!** Ten Christmas characters are hiding on every page in this fun book. Read the profiles below to learn all about their personalities, then look carefully at the scenes to find where each one is hiding. Answers are at the back of the book so you can check your seasonal searching skills!

## SANTA

**HOBBY:**
Writing lists

**MOST EATEN SNACK:**
Christmas cookies

**SECRET SKILL:**
Climbing

## JULIET

**FAVORITE COLOR:**
Green

**HOBBY:**
Taking s-elfies

**FAVORITE RESTAURANTS:**
S-elf service

## JOHN

**KNOWN FOR:**
Elf-confidence

**FAVORITE MUSIC:**
Hip-hop and wrap

**SECRET SKILL:**
S-elf taught
bell ringing

## MARY

**FAVORITE SONG:**
Jingle Bells

**FAVORITE BOOK:**
The Night Before
Christmas

**KNOWN FOR:**
Festive spirit

## MARIAH

**KNOWN FOR:**
Swimming skills

**MOST-USED PHRASE:**
Have a n-ice day!

**FAVORITE HOLIDAY DESTINATION:**
Anywhere n-ice

## ARTHUR

**FAVORITE TREAT:**
Ice pops

**KNOWN FOR:**
Being a cool guy

**MOST-USED PHRASE:**
I'm chilling

## GWEN

**MOST EATEN SNACK:**
Rainbow cake

**FAVORITE WEATHER:**
Rain

**MOST-USED PHRASE:**
Oh, deer!

## KEVIN

**KNOWN AS:**
A high-flier

**FAVORITE SONG:**
Let It Snow!

**FAVORITE SAYING:**
Hoof a great day!

## GEORGE

**FAVORITE STORY:**
Goldilocks and the Three Bears

**KNOWN FOR:**
Cuddly bear hugs

**FAVORITE ACCESSORY:**
Christmas sweater

## SUSAN

**KNOWN AS:**
A snappy dresser

**LOVES:**
Anything sweet

**MOST-USED PHRASE:**
Oh, crumbs!

# TREE-MENDOUS TOWN

It's beginning to look a lot like Christmas in this
snowy town! Where are all the festive friends hiding?

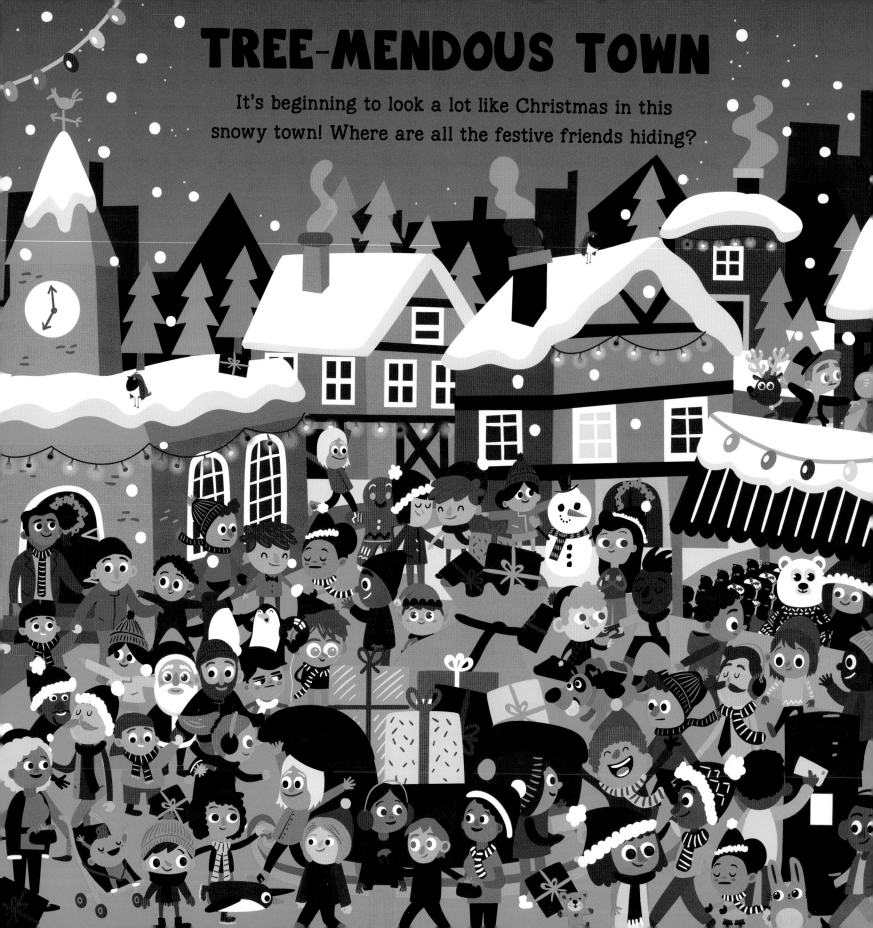

CAN YOU SPOT THE GREEN CANDY CANE?

# MAGICAL TOY SHOP

Santa and his friends are in the toy shop checking that all the children are being good. Can you spot all ten festive pals?

CAN YOU SPOT THE LITTLE BLUE DUCK?

# MERRY COAST-MAS

Search this seaside scene for Santa and his friends
enjoying the sunshine. Look carefully, they're hidden well!

# FESTIVE FAIR

When they are not busy preparing for Christmas, the festive
friends love fairground rides. Can you spot them all?

ENJOY THE RIDES!

CAN YOU SPOT THE RED AND GREEN DRUM?

# THAT'S A WRAP

The presents are being wrapped and loaded on the sleigh.
Try to find all ten characters in this busy scene.

CAN YOU SPOT THE CAMERA?

# SUN, SEA, AND SANTA!

It's time for a break and some fun in the sun.
Can you spot the friends in this busy beach scene?

CAN YOU SPOT THE JAR OF SWEETS?

# FESTIVE FARM

Even the animals on the farm like to celebrate Christmas.
See if you can spot each festive friend in the farmyard.

CAN YOU SPOT
THE RED HAT?

# CHRISTMAS ON ICE

The skates are on and everyone is slipping and sliding on the ice.
The friends are great skaters, but where are they?

CAN YOU SPOT
THE RED MUG?

# SWEET TREATS

Look at all the yummy sweets! The festive friends are
hiding here somewhere. Can you find them all?

CAN YOU SPOT THE RED STOCKING?

# SAFARI SLEIGH RIDE

Uh-oh! It looks like Santa's sleigh has taken a wrong turn and landed in the jungle! Look closely to find all of the festive gang.

CAN YOU SPOT
THE SNOW
GLOBE?

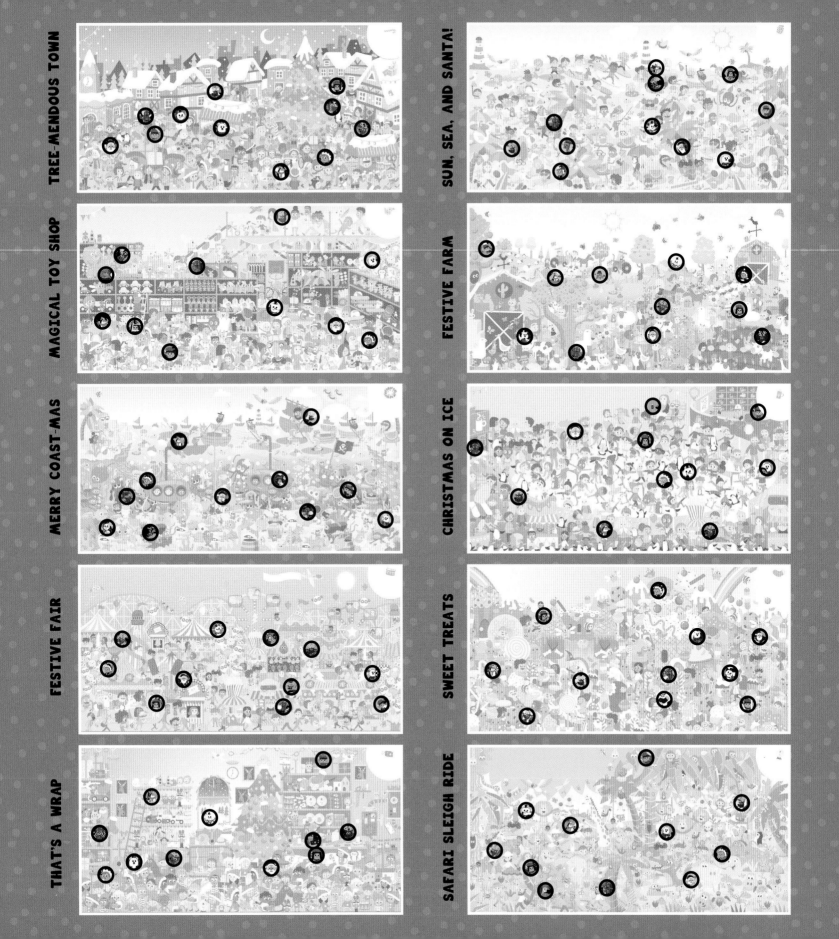

TREE-MENDOUS TOWN

SUN, SEA, AND SANTA!

MAGICAL TOY SHOP

FESTIVE FARM

MERRY COAST-MAS

CHRISTMAS ON ICE

FESTIVE FAIR

SWEET TREATS

THAT'S A WRAP

SAFARI SLEIGH RIDE